# PRO

THE GRA

BASED ON THE BESTSELLING TRILOGY BY

MARIE LU

ADAPTED BY LEIG ... RATED BY KAARI

G.P. PUTNAM'S SONS
An Imprint of Penguin Random House LLC
375 Hudson Street
New York, NY 10014

*Library of Congress Cataloging-in-Publication Data is available.*

Pencils by Kaari
Colored by Kaari, Kate Yan, Angie, Vicki, Depinz, Cindy, and Amelia Tan

Printed in Canada

ISBN 978-0-399-17190-1

10 9 8 7 6 5 4

LAS VEGAS, NEVADA
REPUBLIC OF AMERICA
POPULATION 7,427,431

JAN. 4. 1932 HOURS,
OCEAN STANDARD TIME

35 DAYS AFTER METIAS'S DEATH

HEEEEYYY . . .
WHAT CLUB YOU
FROM, GORGEOUS?

WHUF!

DON'T TOUCH
HER!

NEXT TIME, JUST GO
WITH IT. LAST THING WE
NEED IS A FIGHT.

BE A PRETTY
PATHETIC FIGHT.
HE COULD BARELY
STAND.

WE PLEDGE ALLEGIANCE TO THE FLAG OF THE GREAT REPUBLIC OF AMERICA—

FZZTT
WHAT—
NEVER SEEN THE PLEDGE INTERRUPTED—
THIS ISN'T NORMAL.
—MAYBE THE COLONIES—
COULD IT BE THE WEATHER?
YEAH, SOMETHING BIG'S HAPPENED.
SOME KINDA FREAK ACCIDENT?

WE MUST INSTRUCT ALL SOLDIERS AND CIVILIANS TO REPLACE THE ELECTOR PORTRAITS IN YOUR HOMES.
YOU MAY PICK UP A NEW PORTRAIT FROM YOUR LOCAL POLICE HEADQUARTERS. INSPECTIONS TO ENSURE YOUR COOPERATION WILL COMMENCE IN TWO WEEKS.
THAT'S THE ELECTOR PRIMO'S SON, ANDEN.

THE ELECTOR MUST'VE DIED.
YEAH. AND THE REPUBLIC PRETENDS IT NEVER HAPPENED AND JUST SKIPS AHEAD TO THE NEXT ELECTOR.
HEY! HEY, YOU TWO! WAIT UP!
WELL.
I THOUGHT THAT WAS YOU.

YOU TWO ARE PRETTY STUBBORN IF YOU CAME ALL THE WAY OUT HERE TO FIND US.

HOW IN THE WORLD CAN A GROUP OF CRIMINALS BE LIVING IN ONE OF VEGAS'S LARGEST MILITARY BARRACKS?
WELCOME TO OUR HUMBLE HOME!
WHEEEEEWWW...
DAY!
TESS, IS THAT REALLY YOU?
YOU'RE ACTUALLY HERE! I CAN'T BELIEVE IT!
GLAD TO SEE YOU, COUSIN.
OKAY, ENOUGH. THIS ISN'T THE DAMN OPERA.
SO. YOU MUST BE THE ONE WE'VE ALL HEARD SO MUCH ABOUT. PLEASED TO MEET YOU, DAY.
FLOP
AND YOU MUST BE JUNE IPARIS, THE REPUBLIC'S MISSING PRODIGY.
MY NAME'S RAZOR, AND I CURRENTLY HEAD THE PATRIOTS.

NOW, WHAT BRINGS YOU TWO HERE?

WE NEED YOUR HELP. I CAME TO FIND TESS, BUT I ALSO NEED TO FIND MY BROTHER EDEN. I DON'T KNOW WHAT THE REPUBLIC'S USING HIM FOR OR WHERE THEY'RE KEEPING HIM. WE FIGURED YOU WERE THE ONLY PEOPLE OUTSIDE THE MILITARY WHO MIGHT BE ABLE TO GET INFORMATION.

I'LL BE BLUNT WITH YOU, DAY. THE PATRIOTS AREN'T A CHARITY, AND YOU'RE ASKING FOR A GREAT DEAL OF HELP. YOUR SKILLS ARE NOT AS VALUABLE AS THEY ONCE WERE. OVER THE YEARS, WE'VE RECRUITED OTHER RUNNERS, AND ADDING ANOTHER TO OUR TEAM ISN'T A PRIORITY.

FORTUNATELY, THERE IS SOMETHING YOU CAN OFFER US. AS YOU PROBABLY LEARNED DOWN ON THE STREET, THE FORMER ELECTOR PRIMO DIED TODAY, LEAVING HIS SON, ANDEN, AS THE REPUBLIC'S NEW ELECTOR.

PRACTICALLY A BOY, AND VERY DISLIKED BY HIS FATHER'S SENATORS. RARELY HAS THE REPUBLIC BEEN AS VULNERABLE AS IT IS NOW. THERE WILL NEVER BE A BETTER TIME TO SPARK A REVOLUTION.

I'D BE HAPPY TO TAKE YOU IN AND HELP YOU, DAY. IN RETURN, I WANT YOUR HELP ON A NEW PROJECT.

YOU'LL BOTH NEED TO PLEDGE ALLEGIANCE TO THE PATRIOTS BEFORE I'LL REVEAL ANY DETAILS, HOWEVER.
I'M IN.
ME TOO.
IT'S OFFICIAL, THEN.
THE TWO OF YOU ARE GOING TO HELP US ASSASSINATE THE NEW ELECTOR PRIMO.

MS. IPARIS, YOU'VE MET OUR NEW ELECTOR BEFORE, CORRECT? HE KISSED YOUR HAND?

ONCE, AT AN AWARDS CEREMONY. IT REALLY WASN'T A BIG DEAL.

I'VE HEARD RUMORS THAT ANDEN WAS QUITE TAKEN WITH YOU. THERE'S EVEN A RUMOR THAT HE WANTED YOU TAPPED TO TRAIN AS THE SENATE'S NEXT PRINCEPS.
WHAT'S A PRINCEPS? SOME OF US AREN'T VERSED IN THE REPUBLIC'S HIERARCHY.
THE LEADER OF THE SENATE. THE ELECTOR'S SHADOW. HIS, OR HER, PARTNER IN COMMAND—AND SOMETIMES MORE. ANDEN'S MOTHER WAS THE LAST PRINCEPS, AFTER ALL.
THOSE RUMORS ARE EXAGGERATED, AND EVEN IF THEY WEREN'T, I'D STILL BE ONE OF SEVERAL PRINCEPS-IN-TRAINING.
YOU'RE BLUSHING, IPARIS. DO YOU LIKE THE IDEA THAT ANDEN'S CRUSHIN' ON YOU?
NO.

DON'T BE SO GODDY ARROGANT. ANDEN'S A HANDSOME GUY WITH A LOT OF POWER AND OPTIONS. IT'S OKAY TO FEEL FLATTERED. I'M SURE DAY UNDERSTANDS.

KAEDE, PLEASE.

JUNE, EVEN NOW ANDEN CAN'T BE SURE YOU ACTED AGAINST THE REPUBLIC ON PURPOSE. FOR ALL HE KNOWS YOU WERE TAKEN HOSTAGE WHEN DAY ESCAPED. ANDEN CHOSE TO LIST YOU AS A MISSING PERSON, NOT A WANTED TRAITOR.

HE'S INTERESTED IN YOU.

SO YOU WANT ME TO GO BACK TO THE REPUBLIC?

EXACTLY. YOU TELL THE ELECTOR THAT THE PATRIOTS ARE GOING TO KILL HIM—BUT THE PLAN YOU TELL HIM ABOUT WILL BE A DECOY.

THE WORLD OUTSIDE THE REPUBLIC ISN'T PERFECT, BUT FREEDOMS AND OPPORTUNITIES DO EXIST OUT THERE.

OUR COUNTRY IS ON THE BRINK—ALL IT NEEDS NOW IS A HAND TO TIP IT OVER.

WE CAN BE THAT HAND. WE CAN MAKE IT INTO THE UNITED STATES AGAIN. PEOPLE WILL LIVE FREELY, AND EDEN WILL GROW UP IN A BETTER PLACE.

THAT'S WORTH DYING FOR, ISN'T IT?

DO YOU KNOW HOW LONG THIS'LL TAKE?
A FEW HOURS.
IT'LL BE OVER SOON.

UUUNHHH . . .

HUFF . . .
HUFF . . .
COME ON.
WE'RE IN THIS TOGETHER.

UHH . . .
YOU'RE AWAKE!
YOU'RE— HOW ARE YOU FEELING?
. . .
SLOW.
NOT FOR LONG! SOON YOU'LL BE BETTER THAN NEW AND WE CAN HEAD FOR THE WARFRONT TO KILL THE ELECTOR.
LOOK AT YOUR LEG.

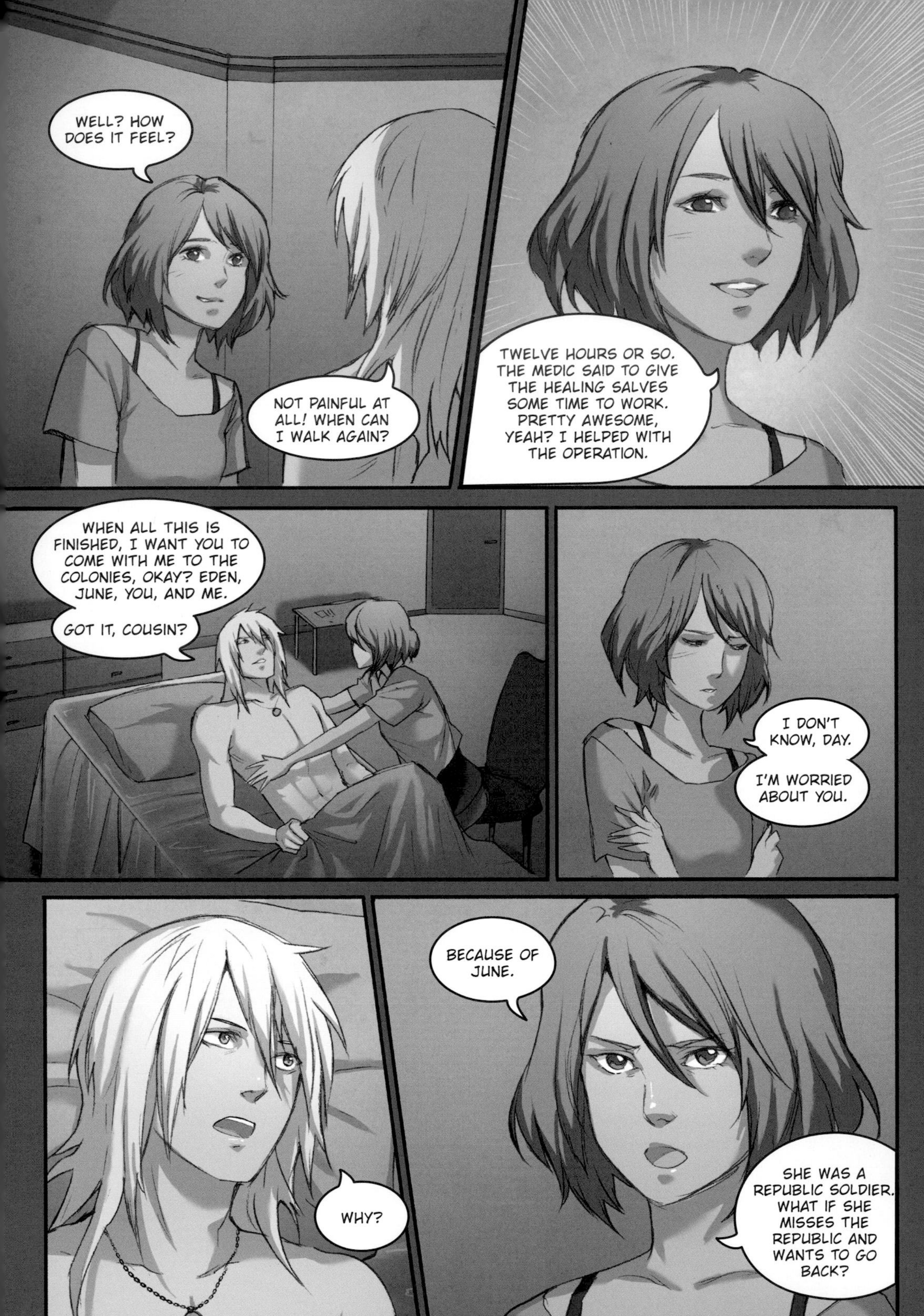
WELL? HOW DOES IT FEEL?
NOT PAINFUL AT ALL! WHEN CAN I WALK AGAIN?
TWELVE HOURS OR SO. THE MEDIC SAID TO GIVE THE HEALING SALVES SOME TIME TO WORK. PRETTY AWESOME, YEAH? I HELPED WITH THE OPERATION.
WHEN ALL THIS IS FINISHED, I WANT YOU TO COME WITH ME TO THE COLONIES, OKAY? EDEN, JUNE, YOU, AND ME.
GOT IT, COUSIN?
I DON'T KNOW, DAY.
I'M WORRIED ABOUT YOU.
WHY?
BECAUSE OF JUNE.
SHE WAS A REPUBLIC SOLDIER. WHAT IF SHE MISSES THE REPUBLIC AND WANTS TO GO BACK?

WHAT IF SHE TRIES TO SABOTAGE—
STOP.
THE REPUBLIC KILLED HER BROTHER. SHE'S NOT LOYAL TO IT ANYMORE.
WE CAN TRUST HER. EVERYTHING WILL BE OKAY. TRUST ME.

DON'T.
DON'T DWELL ON WHO ANDEN IS. DON'T THINK OF HIM AS A REAL PERSON. YOU HAVE TO BE ABLE TO KILL HIM.

HOW IS HE DOING?
GOOD. RIGHT NOW HE'S SITTING UP. HE SHOULD BE ABLE TO WALK IN A COUPLE HOURS.

UM . . .
YOU CAN SEE HIM IF YOU WANT.

HEY.
NOW YOU'LL GET TO SEE ME REALLY RUN A BUILDING. NOT EVEN A BAD KNEE TO HOLD ME BACK.
WHAT ARE YOU DOING?
OH, JUST PASSING THE TIME.
A GIFT FOR YOU.

I KNOW YOU RICH FOLKS HAVE YOUR FANCY TRADITIONS, BUT IN THE POOR SECTORS, GESTURES OF AFFECTION USUALLY GO LIKE THIS.
UNPLATED GALVANIZED STEEL WIRING. THIS IS GOOD MATERIAL, YOU KNOW. STURDIER THAN THE ALLOY ONES, STILL BENDY, STILL . . .
I LIKE IT. I REALLY LIKE IT.
YOU'RE WELCOME.

I HOPE YOU'VE HAD ENOUGH TIME WITH YOUR BOY, MS. IPARIS.
WE MOVE OUT IN HALF AN HOUR. WE HAVE AN AIRSHIP TO CATCH.

STOP TUGGING ON YOUR UNIFORM, YOU'RE MESSING UP THE ALIGNMENT. YOUR DISGUISE NEEDS TO BE PERFECT.

I DON'T KNOW HOW YOU CAN STAND WEARING THIS STUFF ALL THE TIME.

JUNE.

STAY SAFE. I WANT TO SEE YOU AGAIN WHEN ALL THIS IS DONE.

OFFICERS
RS DYNASTY
DEPARTURE:
0851 OCEAN
ARRIVAL:
1704 BORDER STANDARD TIME, BLACKWELL DOCK, LAMAR, CO
GARBAGE

THE GARBAGE CHUTES.
SPOKEN LIKE A TRUE RUNNER.
FICERS

THOMAS!
HE'S HERE FOR JUNE. KEEP MOVING.

COME ON! WE'VE GOT TO GO NOW!
GO ON, MAKE THE FIRST JUMP.
I HOPE THIS KNEE IS WORTH THE MONEY RAZOR PAID FOR IT.
KRIK

WHUMP
HOW'S THE KNEE?
BETTER THAN EVER.

PUT UP A FIGHT WHEN THEY COME FOR YOU. MAKE SURE THEY BELIEVE YOU DON'T WANT TO GET CAUGHT. YOU WERE TRYING TO TURN YOURSELF IN NEAR DENVER, OKAY?
BARRACK 4A
GOT IT.
RAZOR WANTS YOU HERE TO ENSURE THE RIGHT SOLDIERS CAPTURE YOU. HE HAS A SPECIFIC PATROL IN MIND.
BARRACK 4A
KLIK

BARRACK 4A
OLLIE! HE'S ALIVE! HE'S HERE! WHO—
RROW RROWFF!
THOMAS. ONLY HE WOULD THINK TO USE MY OWN DOG TO SNIFF ME OUT.
BARRACK 4A

SIR, ONE OF COMMANDER DESOTO'S MEN JUST CONFIRMED HE SAW HER COME IN HERE.
NO! DON'T FIRE! HOLD YOUR FIRE!

BE CAREFUL, DAMN IT!

GOOD TO SEE YOU AGAIN, MS. IPARIS.

YOU'RE UNDER ARREST FOR ATTACKING REPUBLIC SOLDIERS AND ABANDONING YOUR POST.

HIGH DESERT PENITENTIARY
ROOM 416
WHY AM I BEING HELD HERE?
SHOULDN'T I BE ON MY WAY TO LOS ANGELES?

LOS ANGELES IS UNDER QUARANTINE. ALL OF IT.

ARE THE PLAGUES REALLY THAT BAD RIGHT NOW?

I DON'T WANT TO HURT YOU. IN SPITE OF EVERYTHING YOU'VE DONE, MY HIGHER-UPS STILL CONSIDER YOU TO BE QUITE VALUABLE.
HOW KIND. I'M LUCKIER THAN METIAS.
MS. IPARIS, WHAT HAPPENED TO YOUR BROTHER—
I KNOW WHAT HAPPENED. YOU KILLED HIM.
IT WAS A DIRECT ORDER FROM COMMANDER JAMESON. WHAT DON'T YOU UNDERSTAND ABOUT THAT? YOUR BROTHER BROKE THE LAW, MULTIPLE TIMES!
YOU KILLED HIM IN A DARK ALLEY AND FRAMED DAY FOR IT!
IT WAS THE MOST MERCIFUL WAY FOR HIM TO GO. IF I'D LEFT IT UP TO ANYONE ELSE, THEY'D PROBABLY HAVE TORTURED HIM TO DEATH.

METIAS . . .
QUIT BUGGING ME, JUNE. I DON'T NEED GIRLFRIENDS. I'VE GOT A TROUBLEMAKING BABY SISTER TO TAKE CARE OF.

METIAS WAS IN LOVE WITH YOU.
HE LOVED YOU AND DID SO MUCH FOR YOU, AND YOU STILL KILLED HIM? HOW COULD YOU?
HE DIDN'T GIVE ME ANY OTHER CHOICE.
I TRIED TO PROTECT HIM. I TRIED TO HIDE THE HACKING HE WAS DOING IN THE GOVERNMENT DATABASES, BUT COMMANDER JAMESON FOUND OUT ANYWAY.
I WARNED HIM. YOU CROSS THE REPUBLIC TOO MANY TIMES, EVENTUALLY YOU GET BURNED. STAY LOYAL, STAY FAITHFUL.
BUT HE DIDN'T LISTEN.
NEITHER ONE OF YOU DO.
AT DAY'S EXECUTION, I TRIED TO COME UP WITH A WAY TO STOP COMMANDER JAMESON FROM ARRESTING YOU. BUT YOU MAKE IT SO HARD FOR PEOPLE TO PROTECT YOU, JUNE.
YOU BREAK SO MANY RULES. JUST LIKE METIAS.

EVEN HE HAD TROUBLE LOOKING OUT FOR YOU. WHAT CHANCE DID I HAVE?
I DID CARE FOR HIM, YOU KNOW. BUT I'M ALSO A SOLDIER OF THE REPUBLIC. I DID WHAT I HAD TO DO.
YOU'RE SO TWISTED! I WISH YOU WERE DEAD!
NO, THAT'S NOT TRUE.
I WANT METIAS TO BE ALIVE AGAIN.

LAMAR, COLORADO

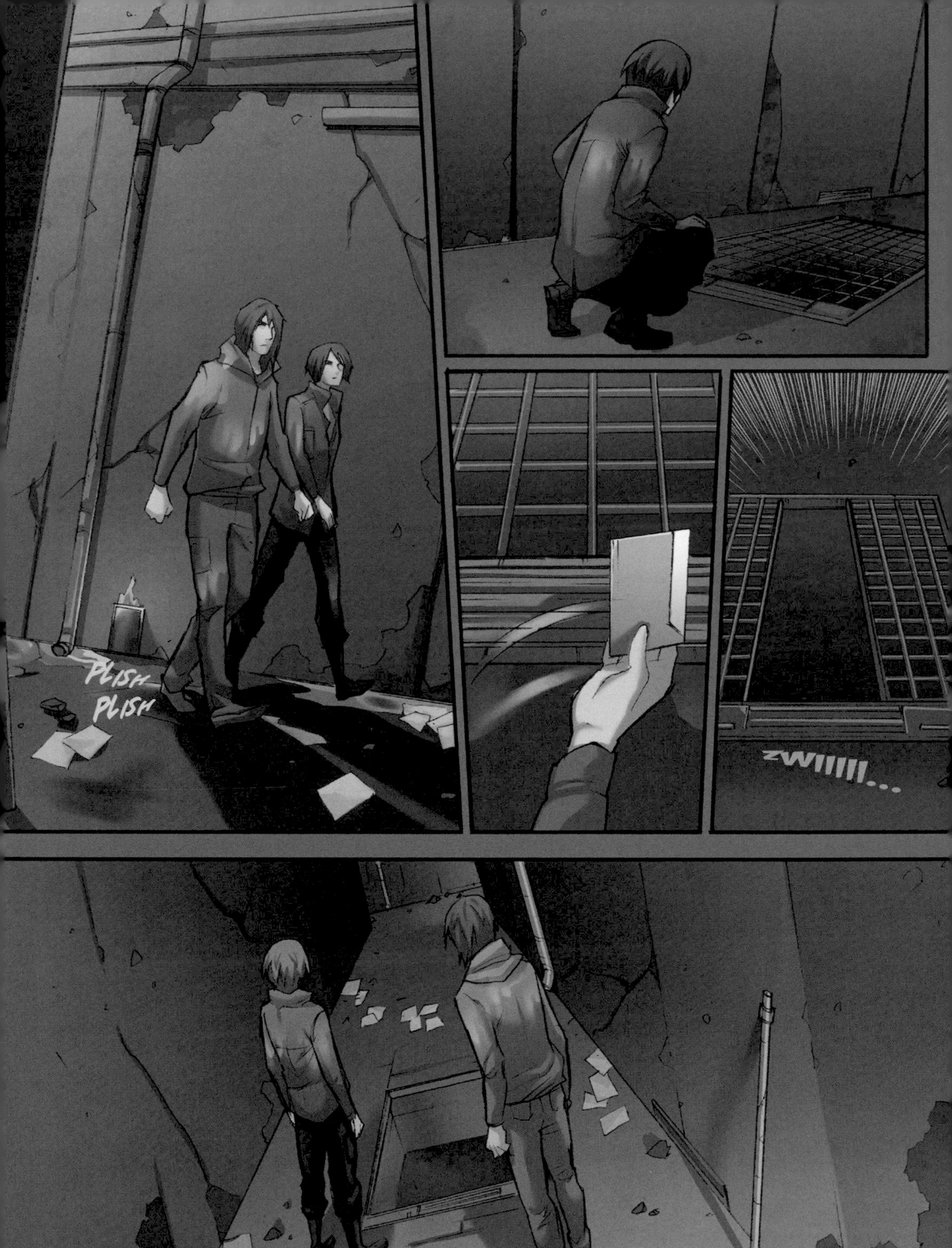
PLISH
PLISH
ZWIIIII...

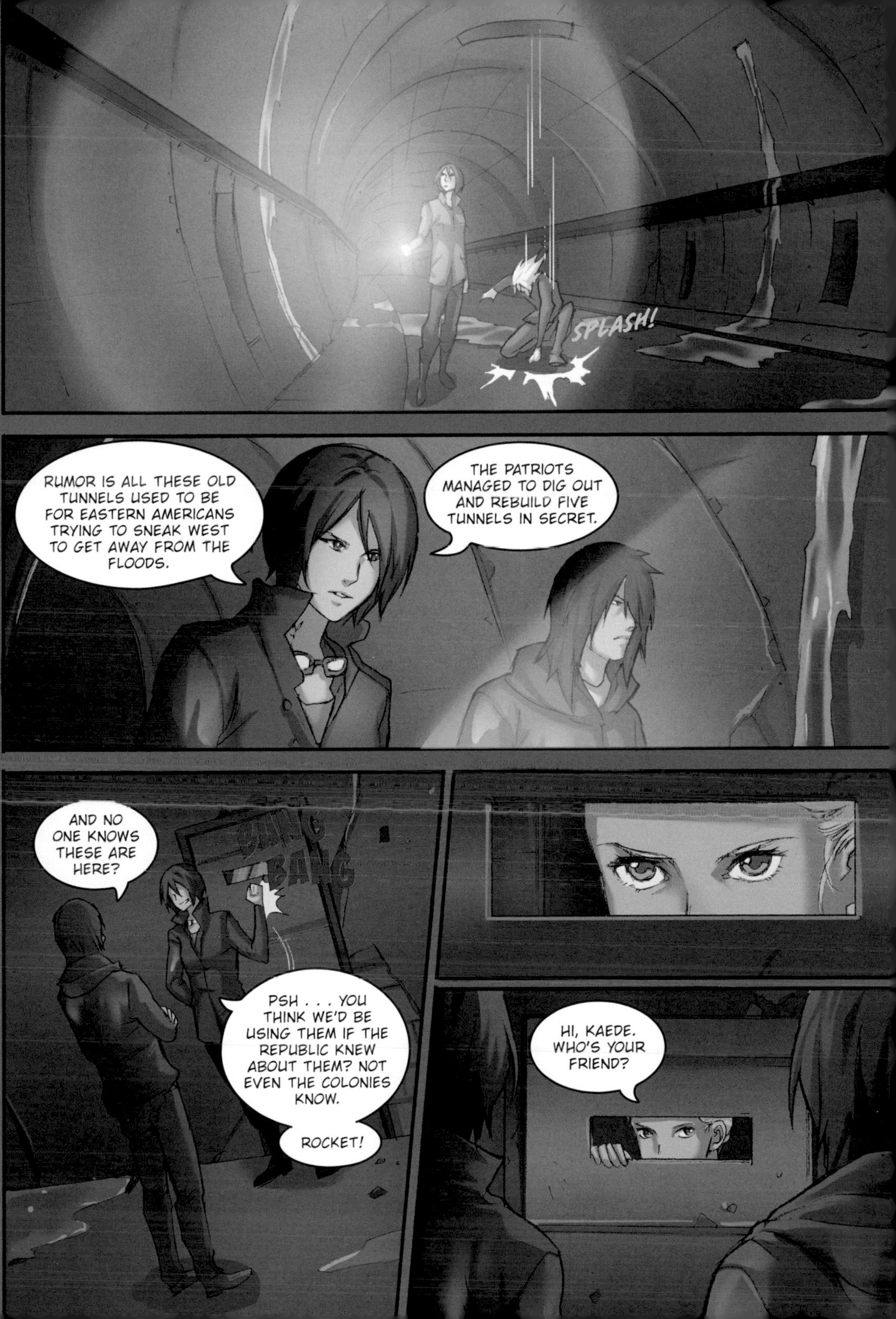

SPLASH!

AND NO ONE KNOWS THESE ARE HERE?

PSH . . . YOU THINK WE'D BE USING THEM IF THE REPUBLIC KNEW ABOUT THEM? NOT EVEN THE COLONIES KNOW.

ROCKET!

HI, KAEDE. WHO'S YOUR FRIEND?

IT'S DAY. NOW LET US IN ALREADY— I'M FREEZING.
ALL RIGHT, JUST CHECKING.
ANY SUDDEN MOVES AND I'LL SHOOT YOU FASTER THAN YOU CAN BLINK.
KNOCK IT OFF.

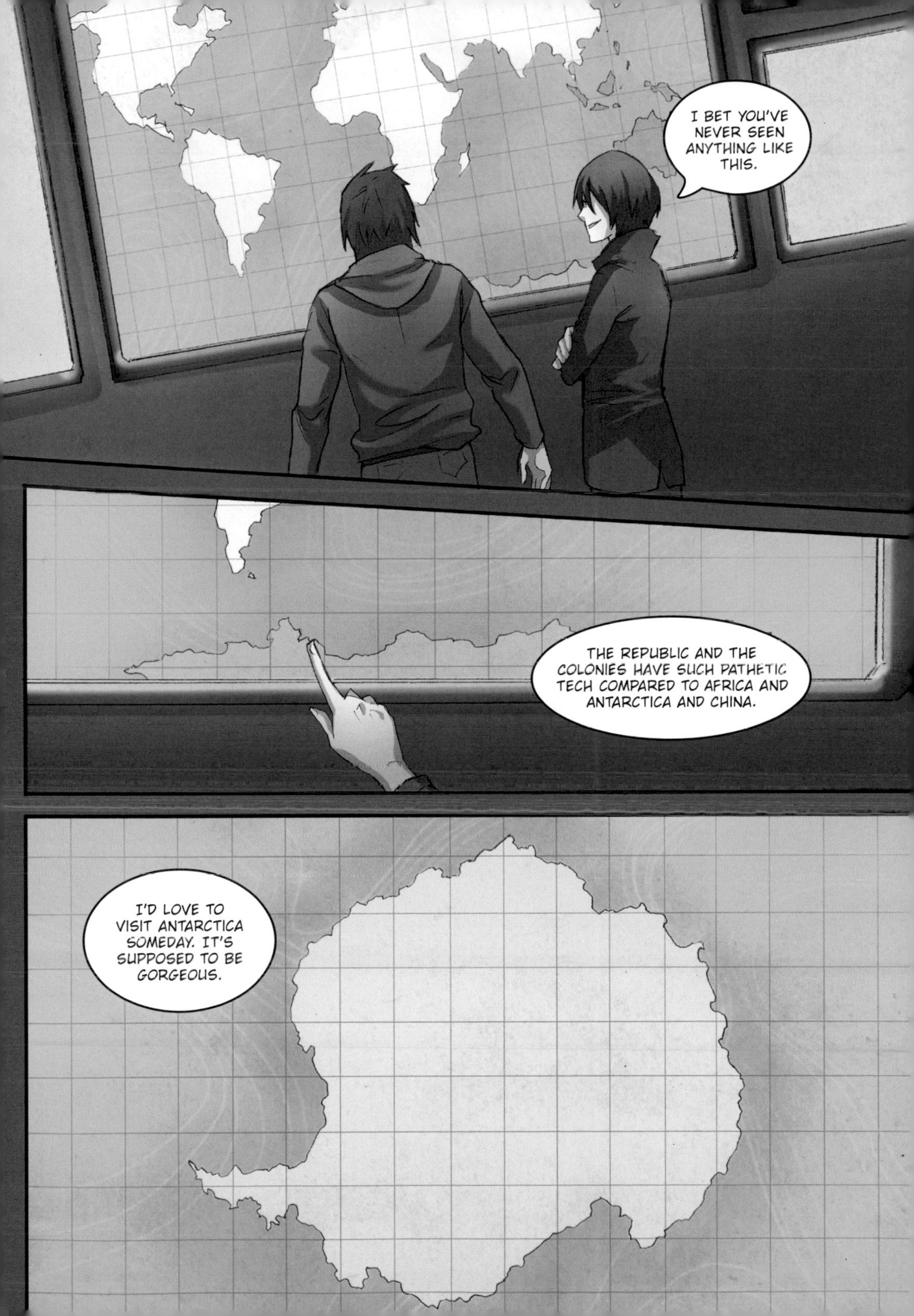
I BET YOU'VE NEVER SEEN ANYTHING LIKE THIS.
THE REPUBLIC AND THE COLONIES HAVE SUCH PATHETIC TECH COMPARED TO AFRICA AND ANTARCTICA AND CHINA.
I'D LOVE TO VISIT ANTARCTICA SOMEDAY. IT'S SUPPOSED TO BE GORGEOUS.

OH, COME ON. IT'S THE REPUBLIC. WHY WOULD THEY?

YOU WANNA SEE THE REPUBLIC FROM A FOREIGN PERSPECTIVE?

—PROPOSED A HALT TODAY TO THE UNITED NATIONS' AID TO THIS HEAVILY MILITARIZED ROGUE STATE UNTIL THERE IS A PEACE TREATY BETWEEN THE ISOLATIONIST COUNTRY AND ITS EASTERN NEIGHBOR—

SO. YOU'RE THE ONE WHO DITCHED TESS, HUH?

SHE BEAT YOU GUYS HERE. SHE'S IN THE MED WARD.

SHUT UP. BAXTER, SHOULDN'T YOU BE GETTING READY FOR TOMORROW NIGHT'S RUN?

WHATEVER. I STILL DON'T UNDERSTAND WHY WE'RE TRUSTING A REPUBLIC-LOVER.

DON'T MIND THAT TROT. BAXTER'S NOT THE BIGGEST FAN OF YOUR GIRL JUNE, BUT STAY ON HIS GOOD SIDE, YEAH? HE'S A RUNNER, TOO.

ANYWAY, DAY, THIS IS PASCAO, THE LEADER OF OUR RUNNERS.

A PLEASURE. I'M YOUR BIGGEST FAN.

**BIGGEST** FAN.

NICE TO MEET ANOTHER RUNNER. I'M SURE I'LL PICK UP SOME NEW TRICKS FROM YOU.
OH, YOU'LL LIKE WHAT'S COMING.
OUR HACKERS SPENT THE LAST FEW WEEKS REWIRING DENVER'S CAPITOL TOWER. NOW WE JUST TWIST A WIRE AND WE'RE BROADCASTING TO THE ENTIRE REPUBLIC.
SOUNDS LIKE FUN. WHAT ARE WE BROADCASTING?
THE ELECTOR'S ASSASSINATION, OF COURSE. WE'RE GONNA RECORD EVERY DETAIL AS WE DRAG HIM OUT OF HIS CAR AND PUT SOME BULLETS IN HIM.
WE'LL DECLARE OUR VICTORY TO THE ENTIRE REPUBLIC OVER THE SPEAKERS.
WANT TO KNOW THE BEST PART?
WHAT?
RAZOR THINKS YOU SHOULD BE THE ONE TO SHOOT THE ELECTOR.

THE CAPITOL
STATION 428

IS DAY ALIVE?

UHN!
KRAK!

KEEP MOVING!
DAY LIVES!
DAY LIVES!
BRING A JEEP AROUND. WE'RE TAKING HER TO COLBURN HALL.
THE ELECTOR'S WAITING.

OUR GLORIOUS
ELECTOR PRIMO.
PLEASE RISE.

PLEASE, SIT. I HOPE YOU'VE BEEN COMFORTABLE, MS. IPARIS.

I HAVE. THANK YOU.

LEAVE US.

ELECTOR, SIR. WE'RE NOT TO LEAVE YOU ALONE.

IT'S ALL RIGHT, CAPTAIN. I'LL BE QUITE SAFE.

YOU CAME HERE TO WARN ME?
YES. I WAS ON MY WAY HERE WHEN I WAS ARRESTED IN VEGAS.
I-I DID HELP DAY ESCAPE HIS EXECUTION, AND THE PATRIOTS HELPED ME. BUT AFTER IT WAS OVER, THEY WOULDN'T LET ME GO.
AND HOW DID YOU GET AWAY FROM THEM? WHERE ARE THEY NOW?
SURELY THEY MUST BE PURSUING YOU.
I MANAGED TO GET AWAY AND HOPPED A VEGAS-BOUND TRAIN THE SAME NIGHT.
THEY'RE PLANNING SOME SORT OF ATTACK AT ONE OF YOUR MORALE-BOOSTING STOPS ALONG THE WARFRONT. LAMAR, WESTWICK, AND BURLINGTON WERE PLACES THEY MENTIONED.
THE PATRIOTS HAVE PEOPLE HERE, ANDEN. PEOPLE IN YOUR INNER CIRCLE.
HOW DO YOU KNOW THIS? DO THE PATRIOTS REALIZE YOU KNOW?
IS DAY INVOLVED IN ALL THIS, TOO?

BECAUSE HE DIDN'T KILL MY BROTHER.

THERE ARE TWO SOLDIERS IN YOUR PERSONAL GUARD WHO ARE GOING TO MAKE AN ASSASSINATION ATTEMPT.

CHINK

MY GUARDS ARE CHOSEN CAREFULLY FOR ME. VERY CAREFULLY.

JUNE.
I WANT TO TRUST YOU . . . AND I WANT YOU TO TRUST ME.
HE KNOWS I'M HIDING SOMETHING.
SIIIGH . . .
WE BOTH UNDERSTAND WHAT IT FEELS LIKE TO LOSE LOVED ONES . . . UNEXPECTEDLY.
I AM NOT THE SAME AS MY FATHER.
CAN I TRUST YOU?
YES.

SO FAR, SO GOOD. RAZOR'LL BE PLEASED. WE'LL HAVE MORE INSTRUCTIONS FOR YOU SOON.

REMEMBER WHO THE ENEMY IS.

SIIIGH . . .
ANDEN . . . HE'S NOT . . . HE DOESN'T SEEM TO BE THE WAY RAZOR DESCRIBED.
CAN I TRUST ANDEN? HELL, FOR THAT MATTER, CAN I TRUST RAZOR?
WHERE IS DAY?

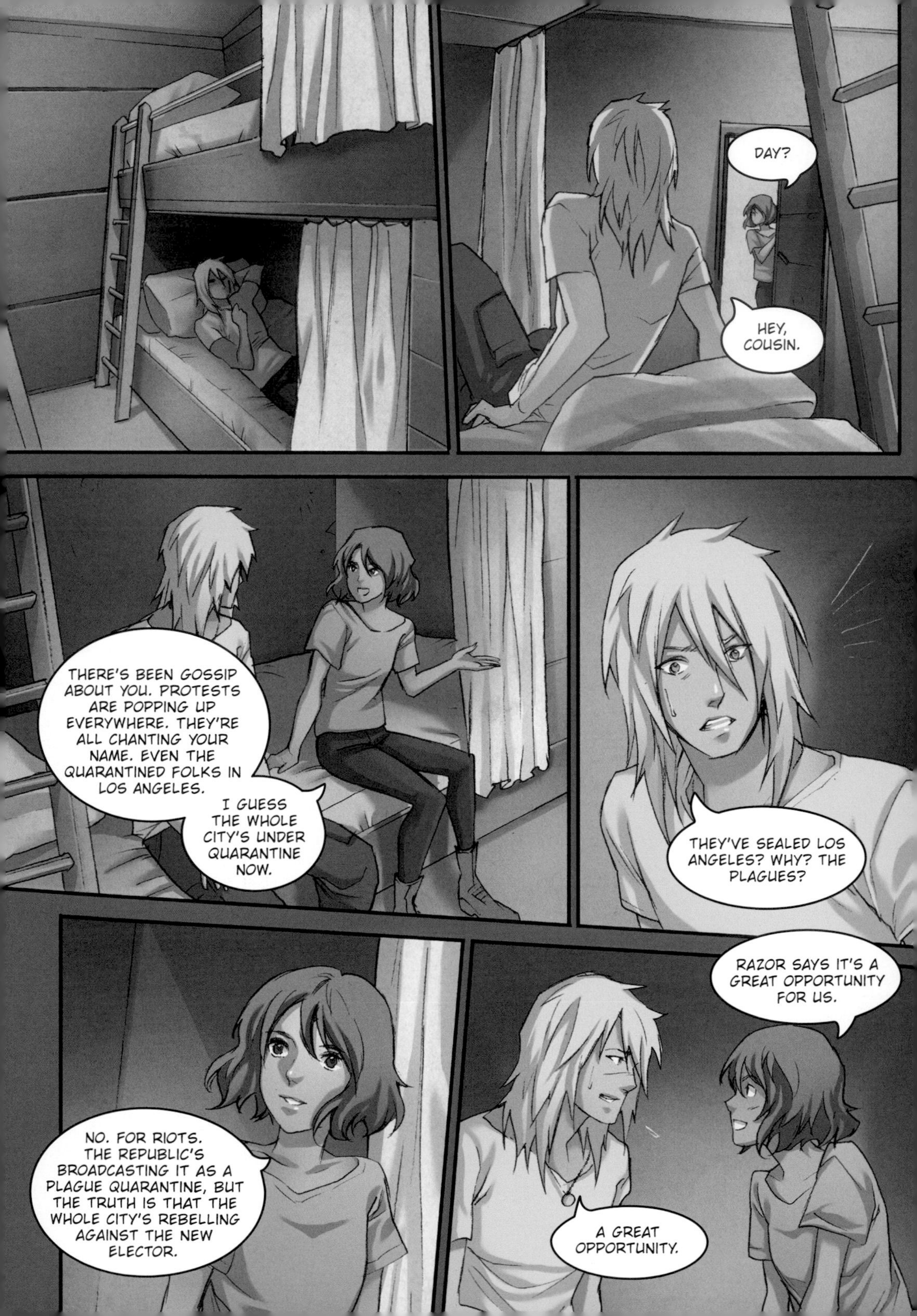

DAY?
HEY, COUSIN.

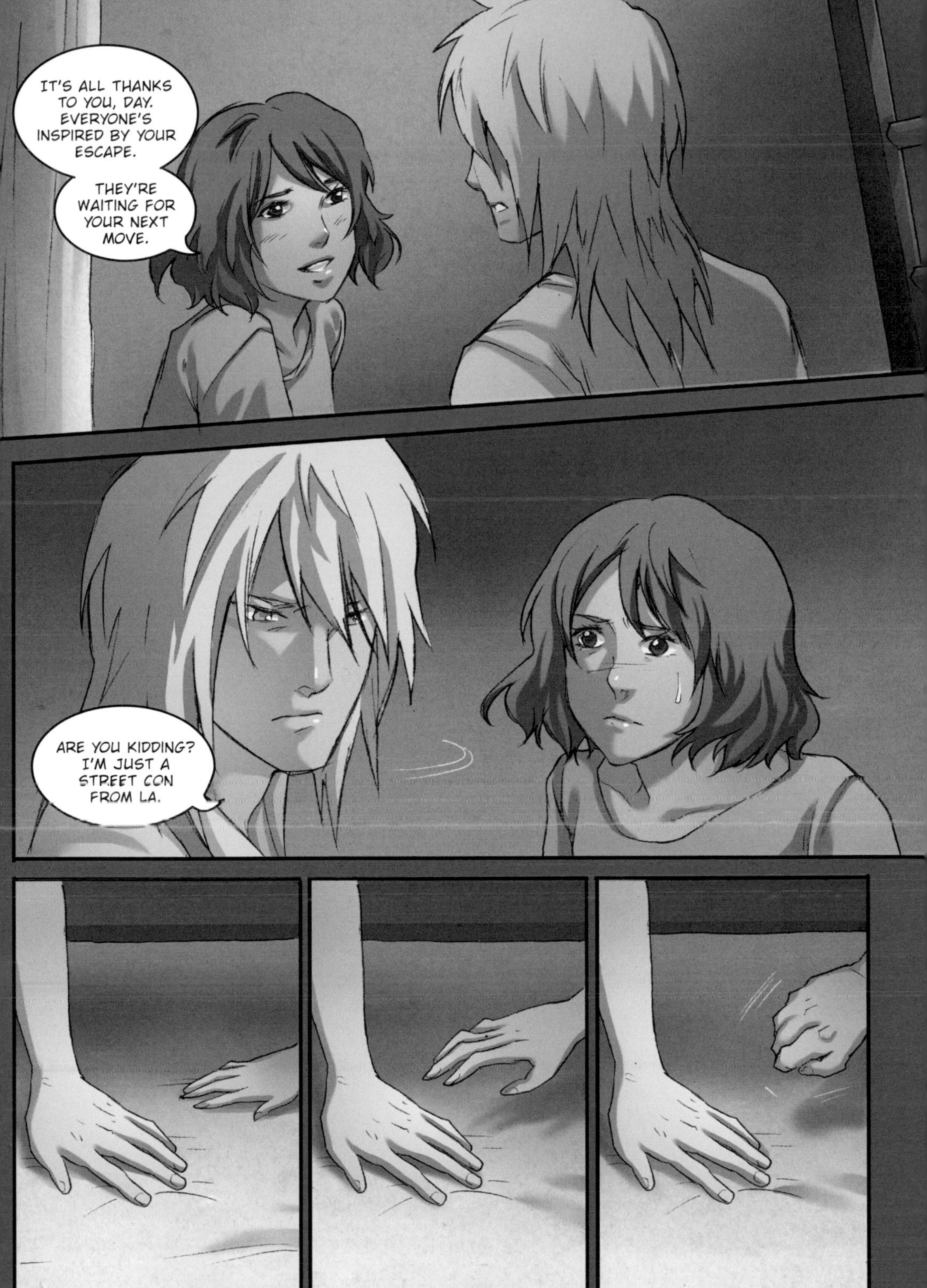
IT'S ALL THANKS TO YOU, DAY. EVERYONE'S INSPIRED BY YOUR ESCAPE.
THEY'RE WAITING FOR YOUR NEXT MOVE.
ARE YOU KIDDING? I'M JUST A STREET CON FROM LA.

YOU REALLY CARE ABOUT THIS ONE, DON'T YOU? SHE'S NOT LIKE THOSE OTHER GIRLS YOU USED TO FOOL AROUND WITH BACK IN LAKE.
WHAT?
IF YOU HAD TO CHOOSE BETWEEN EITHER SAVING ME OR JUNE, WHAT WOULD YOU DO?
I—
WHO WOULD YOU SAVE?!

YOU, ALL RIGHT? I'D SAVE YOU!
WHY?
JUNE WOULDN'T NEED MY HELP.
THANKS FOR YOUR PITY.
TESS, WAIT—I'M SORRY, THAT'S NOT WHAT I—
IT'S FINE. IT'S JUST THE TRUTH, YEAH?
WELL, DON'T WORRY. YOU'LL BE REUNITED WITH JUNE SOON ENOUGH.
IF SHE DECIDES NOT TO GO BACK TO THE REPUBLIC.

UFF!
UHN!
BANG
YOUR PUNISHMENT, MS. IPARIS, FOR WORKING WITH THE ELECTOR.

GASP!
I'D LIKE A PRIVATE WORD WITH MS. IPARIS. IT'LL ONLY TAKE A MINUTE.
ELECTOR, SIR, ARE YOU SURE YOU DON'T WANT A FEW GUARDS WITH YOU—

I'D LIKE TO THANK YOU, JUNE. YOU WERE RIGHT. TWO OF MY GUARDS RAN AWAY THIS AFTERNOON.
THE PATRIOT DECOYS!
I NEED YOUR HELP.
IF YOU HAD A COMPLETE PARDON AND WERE SET FREE, WOULD YOU BE ABLE TO CONTACT DAY?
WHY DO YOU WANT ME TO CONTACT HIM?
YOU AND DAY ARE THE MOST CELEBRATED PEOPLE IN THE REPUBLIC. IF I FORM AN ALLIANCE WITH YOU, I CAN WIN THE PEOPLE.
I'M GOING TO CHANGE THE REPUBLIC, AND I'M GOING TO START BY RELEASING DAY'S BROTHER EDEN.

FIRST OF ALL, I'D LIKE TO REASSURE EVERYONE THAT OUR PLANS ARE ON THE RIGHT TRACK.
OUR AGENT HAS MET WITH THE ELECTOR AND TOLD HIM ABOUT THE DECOY ASSASSINATION PLAN.
SOON THE ELECTOR WILL TRAVEL TO PIERRA, AND A FEW OF OUR SOLDIERS WILL BE ACCOMPANYING HIM.
THERE YOU ARE, HOTSHOT.
YOU, ME, AND A FEW OTHER RUNNERS ARE HEADING OUT IN A COUPLE HOURS.

THERE'S A SHIPMENT COMING INTO LAMAR TONIGHT BY TRAIN. WE'RE GOING TO STEAL SOME SUPPLIES AND THEN BLOW IT UP.
WE'RE GOING TO NEED A SPECIAL RUNNER TO DISTRACT THE SOLDIERS AND GUARDS.
WHAT DO YOU MEAN, SPECIAL?
WHAT I MEAN IS, THIS'LL BE YOUR FIRST CHANCE TO SHOW THE REPUBLIC YOU'RE ALIVE.
WHEN WORD GETS OUT THAT YOU WERE SEEN IN LAMAR, TAKING DOWN A REPUBLIC TRAIN, PEOPLE ARE GOING TO GO NUTS.
OOF!
GO ON, GET READY.
DAY . . .
HEY, I—
WHATEVER.
JUST . . . PROMISE ME YOU'LL BE CAREFUL. I KNOW HOW YOU GET WHEN YOUR ADRENALINE'S PUMPING. DON'T DO ANYTHING TOO CRAZY.

TRAIN ARRIVES IN FIFTEEN MINUTES.
STAY SAFE TONIGHT, OKAY?
BAXTER, IRIS, YOU TWO COME WITH ME.
YOU KNOW THE DRILL.
GOT IT, COUSIN.

WHAT—
TAK
FWOOOM
HEY!

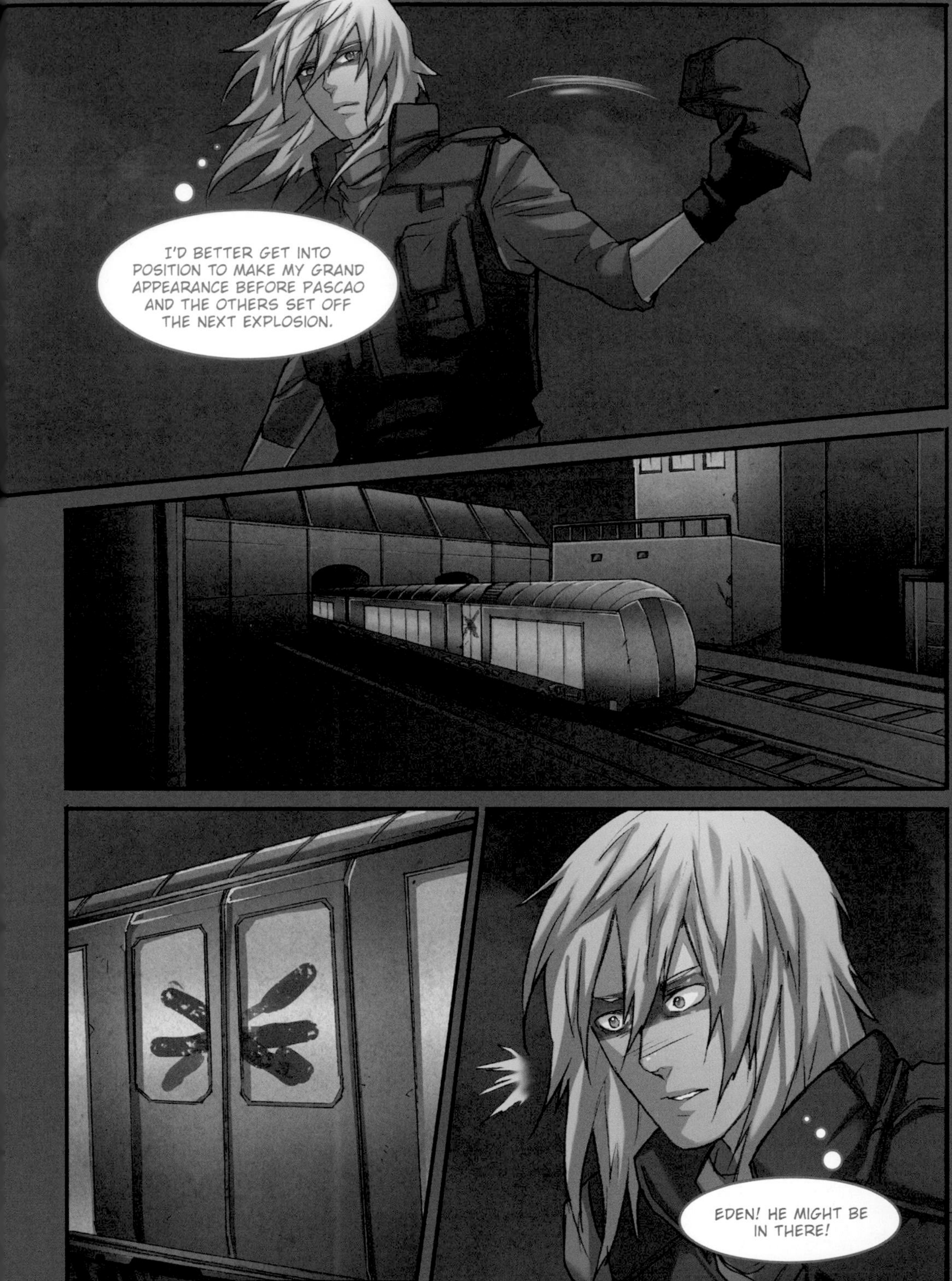

I'D BETTER GET INTO POSITION TO MAKE MY GRAND APPEARANCE BEFORE PASCAO AND THE OTHERS SET OFF THE NEXT EXPLOSION.
EDEN! HE MIGHT BE IN THERE!

TANG
EDEN!
WHACK

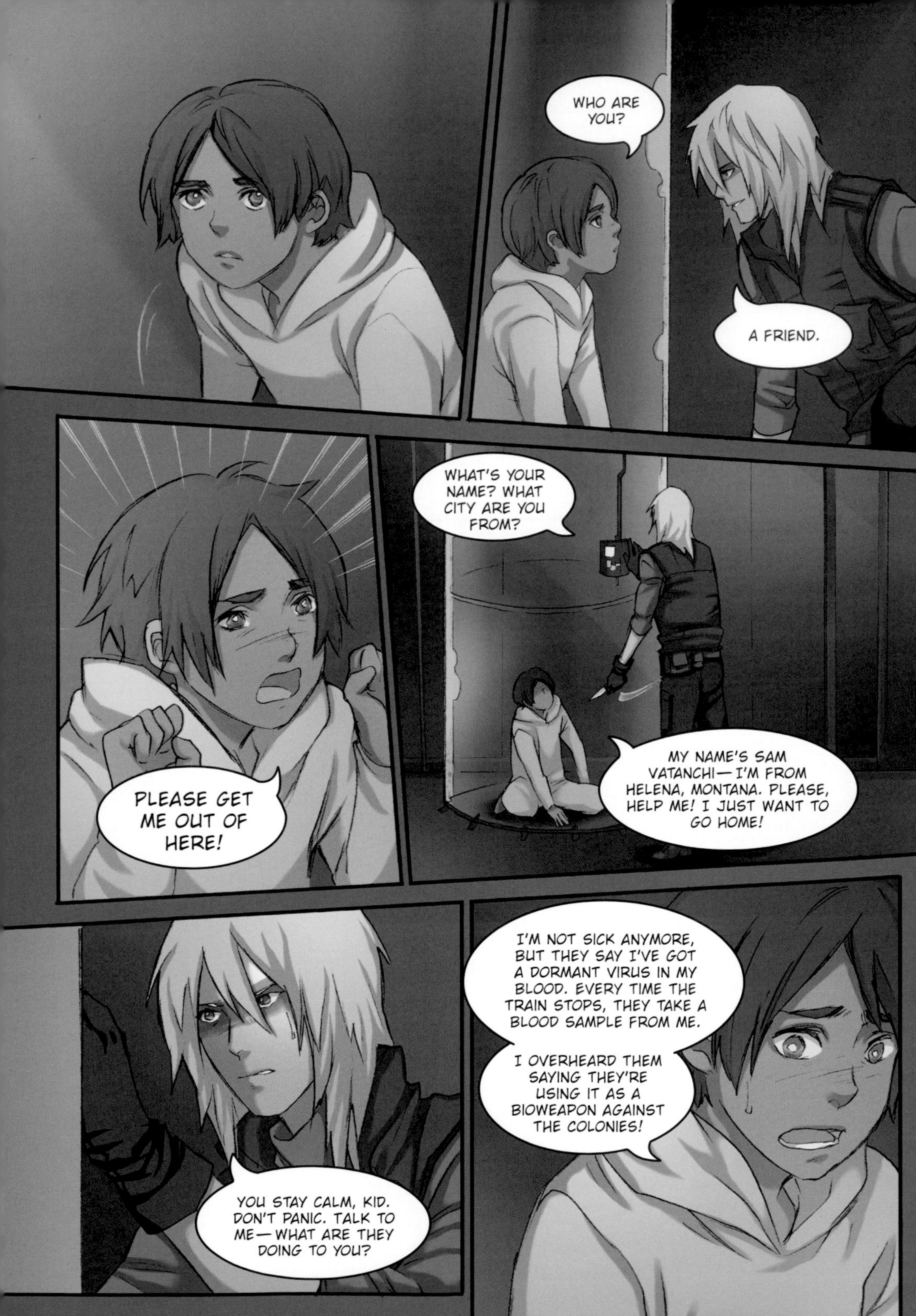
WHO ARE YOU?
A FRIEND.
PLEASE GET ME OUT OF HERE!
WHAT'S YOUR NAME? WHAT CITY ARE YOU FROM?
MY NAME'S SAM VATANCHI— I'M FROM HELENA, MONTANA. PLEASE, HELP ME! I JUST WANT TO GO HOME!
YOU STAY CALM, KID. DON'T PANIC. TALK TO ME— WHAT ARE THEY DOING TO YOU?
I'M NOT SICK ANYMORE, BUT THEY SAY I'VE GOT A DORMANT VIRUS IN MY BLOOD. EVERY TIME THE TRAIN STOPS, THEY TAKE A BLOOD SAMPLE FROM ME.
I OVERHEARD THEM SAYING THEY'RE USING IT AS A BIOWEAPON AGAINST THE COLONIES!

DO YOU KNOW A BOY NAMED EDEN? MAYBE BEING USED LIKE YOU?
NO— I DON'T—
SNAP

WHY THE HELL ARE YOU HERE? YOU WERE SUPPOSED TO MAKE A SCENE ON THE OTHER SIDE OF THE STATION! WHERE WERE YOU?

NOT NOW.

SMAK

I HATE YOU.

I SWEAR I'M GOING TO PUT A BULLET IN YOU THE FIRST CHANCE I GET.

SHHHFFFTTTTT...
I'VE COME TO DELIVER YOUR RELEASE TERMS, JUNE.

ONCE WE ARRIVE IN PIERRA, YOUR RECORD WILL BE SCRUBBED CLEAN, AND I'LL PERSONALLY SEE THAT YOU'RE REINSTATED. I'VE RECOMMENDED YOU FOR A DENVER TEAM.

THANK YOU, ELECTOR.

OH, AND I WANTED YOU TO KNOW THAT YOUR DOG WILL BE WAITING FOR YOU IN THE CAPITOL. I'VE ENSURED HE'S WELL CARED FOR.

BEFORE MY FATHER BECAME ELECTOR, THE TRIALS WERE VOLUNTARY.
HELP US
THE REPUBLIC WAS ORIGINALLY FORMED AFTER FLOODWATERS HAD DESTROYED AMERICA'S EASTERN COASTLINE, AND THE ENTIRE COUNTRY WAS IN A STATE OF TOTAL ANARCHY.
THE FIRST ELECTOR GAVE THE MILITARY UNPRECEDENTED POWER.
THE TRIALS WERE SUPPOSED TO HELP PRODUCE MILITARY-QUALITY CITIZENS, BUT THEN THEY STARTED BEING USED TO WEED OUT THE WEAK AND DEFIANT.

KIDS LIKE DAY . . .
THEN . . . YOU KNOW WHAT HAPPENS TO THE CHILDREN WHO FAIL THEIR TRIAL?
YES. MY FATHER BELIEVED THAT ONLY THE BEST SHOULD SURVIVE. ANYONE ELSE WAS A WASTE OF RESOURCES. AND TO THE SENATE, THE TRIALS ARE A WAY TO REINFORCE THE REPUBLIC'S POWER.
TELL ME. WHAT WOULD YOU DO IF YOU WERE ME? WHAT WOULD YOUR FIRST ACTION BE AS ELECTOR OF THE REPUBLIC?
WIN OVER THE PEOPLE. THE SENATE WON'T HAVE ANY POWER OVER YOU IF THE PUBLIC COULD THREATEN THEM WITH REVOLUTION.
YOU'D MAKE A GOOD SENATOR.

ANDEN WANTS DAY'S HELP . . . MY HELP . . . WE CAN ALL WORK TOGETHER!

ANDEN . . .

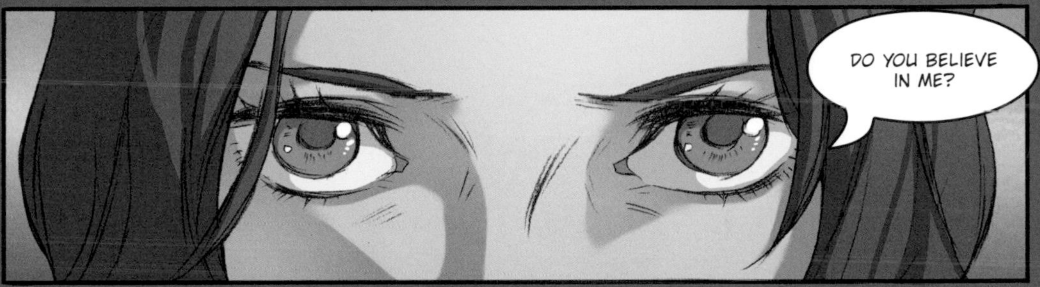
DO YOU BELIEVE IN ME?

YES.
THEN DO WHAT I SAY WHEN WE GET TO PIERRA. PROMISE?

EVERYTHING I SAY.

DAY
LIVES

GO SEE IF KAEDE NEEDS ANY HELP PACKING UP. WE'LL BE LEAVING FOR PIERRA IN ANOTHER HOUR OR SO.

*UHN!*

MAKE SOME ROOM.

JUST STAY THE HELL OUT OF MY WAY.

*HUMPH*. YOU'RE TOUCHY. JEALOUS YOUR GIRL'S WHORING AROUND WITH THE ELECTOR?

YOU'RE AN IDIOT FOR BELIEVING IN THIS REPUBLIC-LOVER, LITTLE GIRL.
THWACK
RAAAR!!!
CRACK
YOU AIN'T ONE OF US!

UHN!
UHN!!
I BET YOU DETOURED OUR TRAIN MISSION ON PURPOSE!
I'M GOING TO SKIN YOU ALIVE, YOU DIRTY DAMN TROT!
TESS, TAKE CARE OF DAY! WE'RE ON A SCHEDULE HERE.
BAXTER, STOP IT! BACK OFF!
I TOLD YOU, I'M FINE. I'VE JUST GOT A BAD HEADACHE.

FEEL NAUSEOUS?
NO. JUST SORE. AND ANGRY.
HEY, COUSIN . . . I'M SORRY ABOUT WHAT I SAID. YOU DON'T NEED ME TO TAKE CARE OF YOU.
!!!
I CAN'T, TESS.

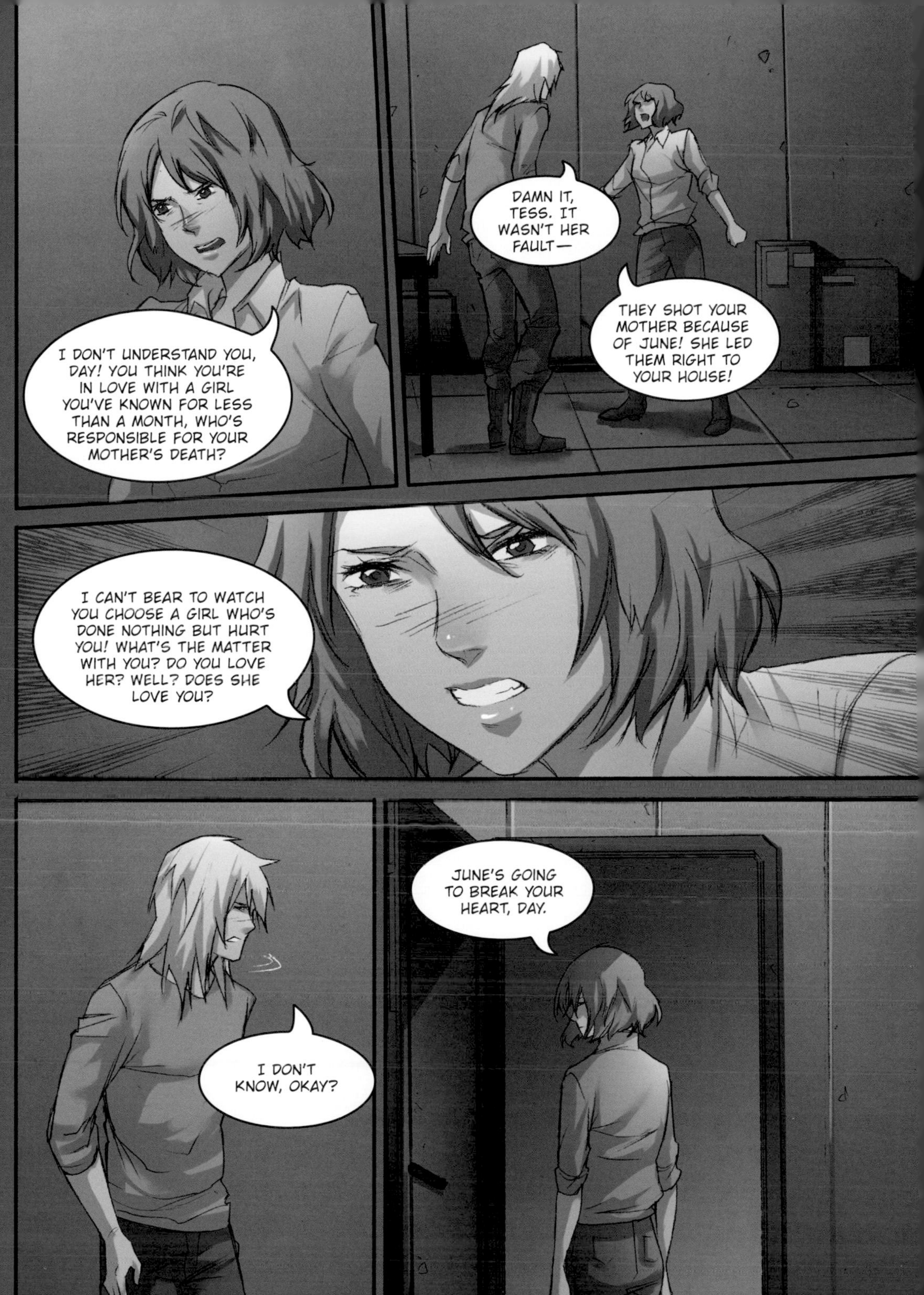
DAMN IT, TESS. IT WASN'T HER FAULT—
THEY SHOT YOUR MOTHER BECAUSE OF JUNE! SHE LED THEM RIGHT TO YOUR HOUSE!
I DON'T UNDERSTAND YOU, DAY! YOU THINK YOU'RE IN LOVE WITH A GIRL YOU'VE KNOWN FOR LESS THAN A MONTH, WHO'S RESPONSIBLE FOR YOUR MOTHER'S DEATH?
I CAN'T BEAR TO WATCH YOU CHOOSE A GIRL WHO'S DONE NOTHING BUT HURT YOU! WHAT'S THE MATTER WITH YOU? DO YOU LOVE HER? WELL? DOES SHE LOVE YOU?
JUNE'S GOING TO BREAK YOUR HEART, DAY.
I DON'T KNOW, OKAY?

HOW LONG WILL THIS TAKE?

NOT LONG, MS. IPARIS.

JUNE IPARIS.
CONGRESS HAS PARDONED YOU OF ALL CRIMES AGAINST THE REPUBLIC, ON THE UNDERSTANDING YOU WILL CONTINUE TO SERVE YOUR NATION TO THE BEST OF YOUR CAPABILITIES.

ANY COMMENTS, SENATORS?
UNDERSTAND YOU ARE NOT YET IN THE CLEAR, AGENT IPARIS. YOU WILL BE WATCHED AT ALL TIMES.
THANK YOU, ELECTOR. THANK YOU, SENATORS.
WELL, NOW THAT THAT'S TAKEN CARE OF, SHALL WE?

I'VE GOT TO DO SOMETHING TO THROW OFF THE PATRIOTS' TIMETABLE . . .
MS. IPARIS? ARE YOU ALL RIGHT?
JUNE!
UHHNN . . .

ELECTOR, SIR, PLEASE STAY BACK. WE'LL TAKE CARE OF THIS.
SHE COULD HAVE THE PLAGUE.

TAKE HER TO THE HOSPITAL. IMMEDIATELY.

YES, ELECTOR.
GOOD—THE HOSPITAL IS IN THE EXACT OPPOSITE DIRECTION FROM THE ORIGINAL ROUTE.
I'LL FOLLOW IN MY CAR.
THE PATRIOTS WON'T HAVE TIME TO ADJUST THEIR POSITIONS.
MAKE SURE YOU BELT HER IN.

HEY, CHAUFFEUR! YOU'RE GOING THE WRONG WAY. HOSPITAL'S ON THE OTHER SIDE OF TOWN.

NEGATIVE. WE JUST GOT ORDERS TO STAY OUR ORIGINAL COURSE.
COMMANDER DESOTO SAYS THE ELECTOR WANTS US TO TAKE MS. IPARIS TO THE HOSPITAL AFTERWARD.

RAZOR! HE MUST BE LYING TO ANDEN'S DRIVER.

EVERYONE'S IN
POSITION.

FIFTEEN MINUTES UNTIL SHOWTIME.
IN FIFTEEN MINUTES THE ELECTOR'S GOING TO BE DEAD . . . BY MY HAND.
WHAT THEN?
A NEW GOVERNMENT. A NEW ORDER.

AS IF I KNOW WHAT'S REALLY GOING TO HAPPEN TODAY.
Bzzzz
—ORANGE AND ECHO STREETS, CLEAR—
DAY?
I'M HERE, PASCAO.
BAXTER'S GETTING READY FOR THE FIRST EXPLOSION.
WHEN THE ELECTOR'S JEEP REACHES HIS STREET, HE'LL TOSS HIS GRENADE.
JUNE WILL SEPARATE THE ELECTOR'S CAR FROM THE OTHERS.
I TOSS MY GRENADE, TURN 'EM RIGHT DOWN YOUR STREET. THEN YOU TOSS YOURS, BOX 'EM IN, AND HEAD DOWN TO THE GROUND.
GOT IT?
YEAH, GOT IT.

REMEMBER EDEN. REMEMBER SAM VATANCHI. YOU CAN DO THIS.
THE CONVOY'S LATE.
SOMETHING MUST'VE HAPPENED. NO MATTER WHAT TESS THINKS, JUNE WOULD NEVER BETRAY US, NOT AFTER WHAT THE REPUBLIC DID TO METIAS.
WHAT IF SOMEONE'S TIPPED THEM OFF?
THEY'D EXECUTE JUNE WITHOUT A SECOND THOUGHT.

STAND BY. WE'VE GOT A DELAY.

THAT WAS ONLY TWO BLOCKS AWAY. I'M NEXT.

STEADY . . .
JUNE . . . WHERE ARE YOU?

JUNE! SHE DOESN'T WANT—
IGNORE JUNE! STAY THE COURSE!
NO . . . JUNE . . . YOU CAN'T STOP NOW.
DAY! DO YOU HEAR ME? STAY THE COURSE!

DAY, NO! WHAT ARE YOU—
!!!

BOOOOM
SKREEEEEE
UHN!

KOF KOF
ANDEN!

BOOOOOM
MAN, IF THE SOLDIERS DON'T KILL US, THE PATRIOTS WILL.
WE'VE GOT TO GET OUT OF HERE!
BARRICADE THE STREET! PROTECT THE ELECTOR!
GET THE ELECTOR OUT OF THIS CAR—THEY'RE GOING TO BLOW IT UP!

YOU!
UHN!
GET TO SAFETY! BEFORE THE OTHERS FIND YOU!

TESS!
COME ON! WE DON'T HAVE MUCH TIME!
NO, DAY. I CAN TAKE CARE OF MYSELF.
DON'T FOLLOW ME.

WE CAN REST HERE. I STAYED IN ONE OF THESE IN LAMAR.

WHAT IF THE PATRIOTS FIND US? THIS IS THEIR HIDEOUT, RIGHT?

the only way out is death
—Mario Márquez

THIS SPOT'S PRETTY OUT OF THE WAY, AND I DON'T THINK THEY'LL BE EXPECTING US TO HIDE OUT RIGHT UNDER THEIR NOSES.

WHAT ABOUT TESS? SHE DIDN'T LOOK TOO HAPPY. SHE MIGHT TELL THEM WE CAME DOWN HERE.

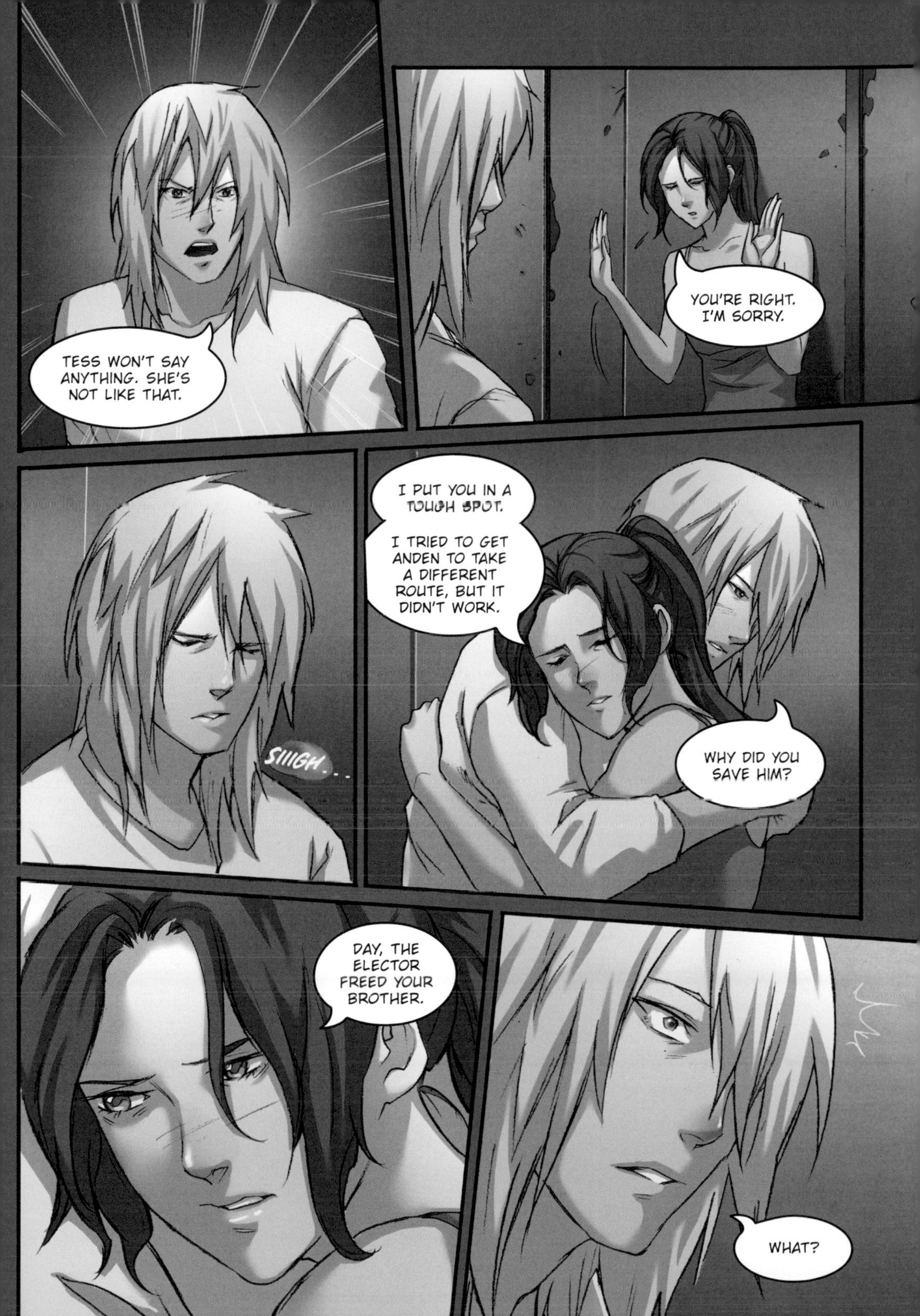
TESS WON'T SAY ANYTHING. SHE'S NOT LIKE THAT.
YOU'RE RIGHT. I'M SORRY.
SIIIGH...
I PUT YOU IN A TOUGH SPOT.
I TRIED TO GET ANDEN TO TAKE A DIFFERENT ROUTE, BUT IT DIDN'T WORK.
WHY DID YOU SAVE HIM?
DAY, THE ELECTOR FREED YOUR BROTHER.
WHAT?

EDEN'S UNDER FEDERAL PROTECTION IN DENVER.
ANDEN'S COMPLETELY OPPOSED TO THE LATE ELECTOR'S POLITICS. HE WANTS TO MAKE A BUNCH OF RADICAL CHANGES, BUT HE NEEDS THE PUBLIC'S SUPPORT FIRST. HE PRACTICALLY BEGGED ME FOR OUR HELP.
THAT'S IT?
THAT'S WHY WE BETRAYED THE PATRIOTS? SO THE ELECTOR CAN BRIBE ME IN EXCHANGE FOR MY SUPPORT?
DAY, PLEASE, YOU HAVE TO BELIEVE ME. ANDEN'S DIFFERENT.
OH? HOW DO YOU KNOW HE'S TELLING THE TRUTH? DO YOU HAVE ANY PROOF HE'S RELEASED EDEN?
NO. I DON'T.
HE PLAYED YOU. YOU, OF ALL PEOPLE.
THE LAST THING THIS COUNTRY NEEDS IS A NEW ELECTOR. THE REPUBLIC IS BROKEN. KILL ANDEN. LET THE COLONIES TAKE OVER.

THAT WON'T FIX THINGS!
AFTER EVERYTHING THIS GOVERNMENT'S DONE TO YOU, EVERYTHING THEY'VE TAKEN FROM YOU—HOW CAN YOU NOT WANT TO SEE THE REPUBLIC COLLAPSE?
I WANT TO SEE IT CHANGE FOR THE BETTER!
HAH!
SO NOW YOU THINK THIS GODDY RICH BOY CAN SAVE US ALL?
IT'S HIS IDEAS THAT MATTER, NOT HIS MONEY! MONEY DOESN'T MEAN ANYTHING WHEN—
MONEY DOESN'T MATTER?! MONEY IS EVERYTHING!
IF YOU'D SPENT YOUR LIFE DIGGING UP TRASH TO EAT IN THE SLUMS, YOU WOULDN'T BE SO QUICK TO JUMP BACK IN ANDEN'S POCKET!
THAT'S NOT FAIR, DAY. I DIDN'T CHOOSE TO BE BORN INTO THIS. I NEVER WANTED TO HURT YOUR FAMILY.

WELL, YOU DID.
YOU LED THE SOLDIERS RIGHT TO MY DOOR. YOU'RE THE REASON MY FAMILY'S DEAD.
BEEP BEEP BEEP BEEP BEEP BEEP BEEP BEEP BEEP BEEP BEEP BEEP BEEP BEEP BEEP BEEP
WHAT—
IT'S TIME TO GO.
ARE THEY STILL FOLLOWING US?
NO. WE LOST THEM A WHILE AGO.

HEY. ARE YOU ALL RIGHT?
YEAH. I THINK I PICKED UP A BUG OR SOMETHING. NOTHING BIG.

YOU'RE BURNING UP.
I'LL BE FINE. COME ON.
HRRRRRRRRRMMMMMMMMMMMMMM

WE MUST BE GETTING CLOSE TO THE OUTSIDE. I SMELL FRESH AIR.

IS THAT AN AIRSHIP OUT THERE?

*HSST!*

WE MUST BE IN
THE COLONIES.

DAILY FOOD

TRIBUNE POLICE DEPARTMENT
NEED TO REPORT A CRIME?
ONLY 500 NOTE DEPOSIT NEEDED!
TRIBUNE POLICE DEPARTMENT
IS A SUBSIDIARY OF DESCON CORP

THE COLONIES OF AMERICA
CLOUD.MEDITECH.DESCON.EVERGREEN
A FREE STATE IS A CORPORATE STATE

HEY—YOU OKAY?
I-I THINK I NEED TO SIT DOWN. I FEEL DIZZY.

JUST A LITTLE FARTHER. WE'LL FIND A HOSPITAL. THERE MUST BE ONE, THIS CLOSE TO THE WARFRONT.

YOU'RE NOT SHOWING UP.

WHICH CORP DO YOU BELONG TO?
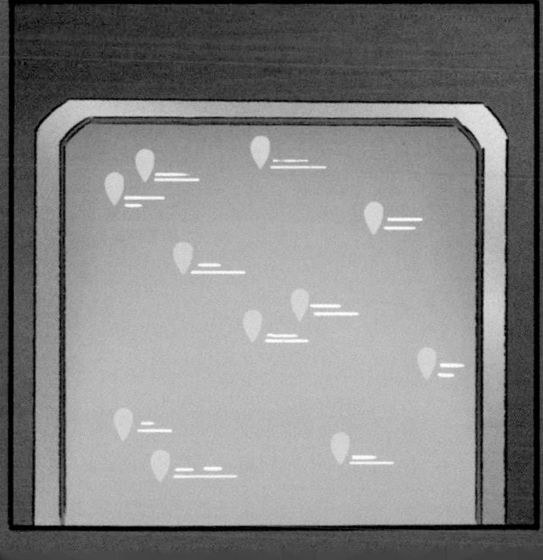

DESCON!

YOU MUST BE NEW.

I'M SPONSORED BY CLOUD CORP. STOP IN TRIBUNE CENTRAL SQUARE TO BUY OUR NEWEST LINE OF BREAD!

TH-THERE'S SOMETHING OFF ABOUT THIS CITY.
YEAH.

COME ON, JUNE. JUST A LITTLE BIT FARTHER.
JUNE!
UUUHHNNN!
I TOLD YOU, WE'RE REFUGEES. WE GOT IN THROUGH THE TUNNELS.

PLEASE, SHE'S BURNING UP WITH FEVER. TAKE US TO A HOSPITAL AND I'LL TELL YOU ANYTHING YOU WANT.

HOSPITAL'S GOING TO COST YOU, SON.

—FROM THE REPUBLIC! I RECOGNIZE HIM!

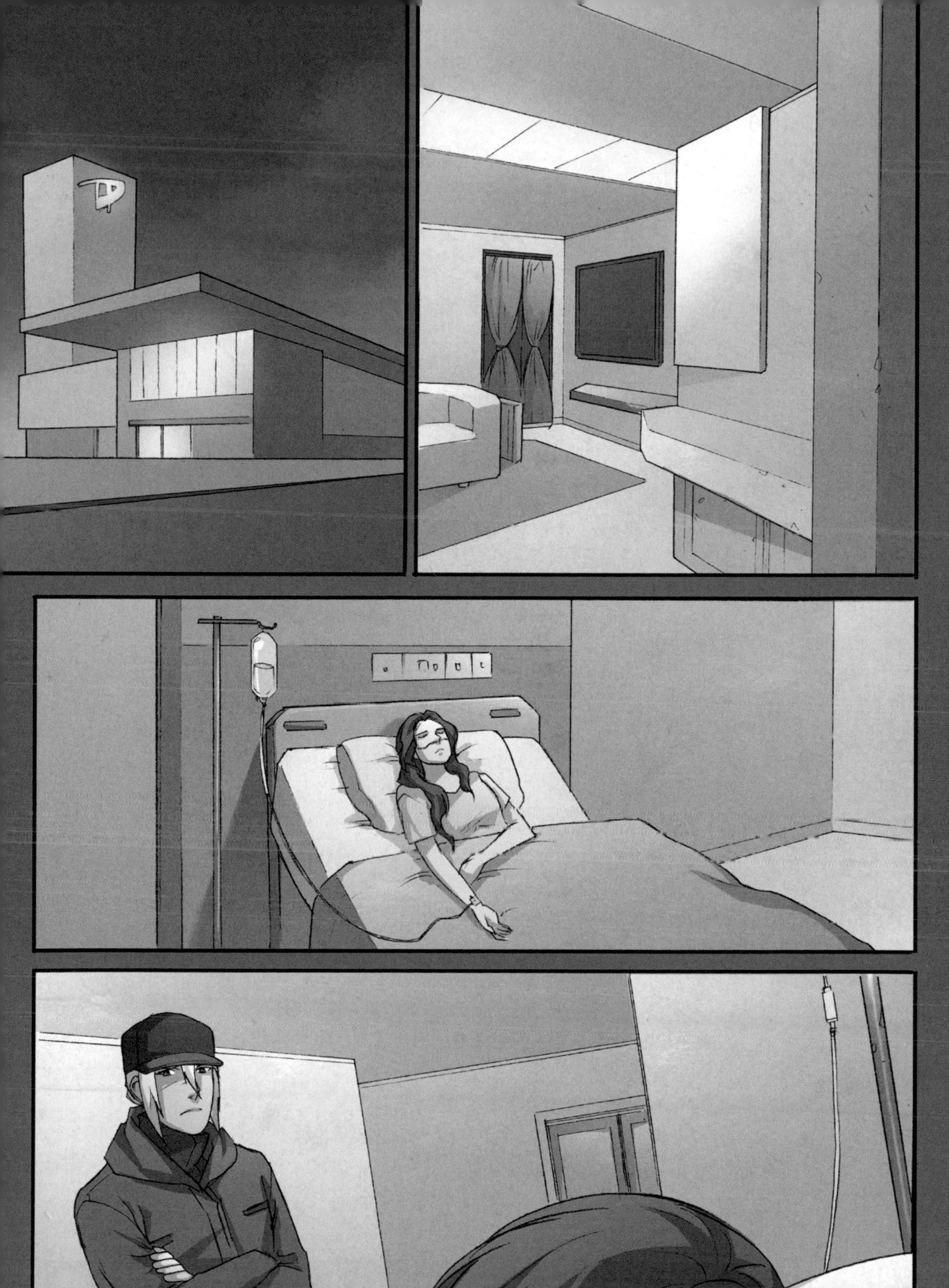

YOUR FRIEND IS STABLE?
YES. THANK YOU.

YOU'RE DANIEL ALTAN WING, RIGHT? EVERGREEN ENT KEEPS PRINTING STORIES ABOUT YOU IN ITS TABS—THE REPUBLIC REBEL, THE PHANTOM, THE WILD CARD!
THEY SAID YOU ESCAPED LOS ANGELES PRISON ALL BY YOURSELF! HEY, DID YOU REALLY DATE THAT SINGER, LINCOLN?
AHAHAHAHAHA!!!
HEH!
OH, AHAHA, I'M SORRY, YOU GUYS KEEP UP ON REPUBLIC PROPAGANDA SINGERS?
LINCOLN'S A LITTLE OLD FOR ME, DON'T YOU THINK?
I CAN'T BELIEVE YOU KNOW SO MUCH ABOUT ME.

C'MERE.

SEE FOR YOURSELF.

DAY!

DAY!

DAY!

YOU'RE A CELEBRITY HERE!
KAEDE!

DON'T WORRY, I'LL MAKE SURE NONE OF YOUR FANS COME BARGING IN.

HEY.

WHAT ARE YOU DOING HERE? DID YOU FOLLOW US THROUGH THE TUNNEL?

YES. I NEED TO WARN YOU.

RAZOR PLAYED US ALL. HE LIED TO THE PATRIOTS, THEN HANDED US OVER TO THE REPUBLIC.

DON'T WORRY—OUR TESS GOT AWAY. SO DID PASCAO AND BAXTER.
ONE OF OUR HACKERS DISCOVERED THAT THE SENATE IS SPONSORING THE PATRIOTS. RAZOR MADE A DEAL WITH THEM—ONCE ANDEN'S DEAD, HE GETS TO BE THE NEW ELECTOR. THEY FIGURED THEY COULD USE THE PATRIOTS TO KILL ANDEN AND THEN PIN THE BLAME ON US.
BUT THEY FAILED. ANDEN'S STILL ALIVE.
FOR NOW. RIOTS ARE BREAKING OUT. CONGRESS IS JUST GOING TO SIT BACK AND LET ANDEN GET KILLED, THEN REPLACE HIM WITH RAZOR.
LET THE REPUBLIC GO HELL! THE COLONIES'LL ROBABLY TAKE OVER.
DO YOU REALLY THINK THINGS WILL BE MUCH BETTER IF THAT HAPPENS? I GREW UP HERE. NO ONE DOES ANYTHING FOR ANYONE UNLESS THEY'VE GOT MONEY OR CAN MAKE MONEY FOR SOMEONE. THEY'RE ONLY HELPING YOU AND JUNE BECAUSE YOU'RE FAMOUS AND THEY THINK THEY CAN USE YOU.

ELECTOR FREES YOUNGER BROTHER OF NOTORIOUS REBEL "DAY"

HE RELEASED ALL OF THE KIDS BEING SENT TO THE WARFRONT, NOT JUST EDEN.
THE SPEAKERS AT THE CAPITOL TOWER, THE ONES THE PATRIOT HACKERS REWIRED—ARE THEY STILL HOOKED UP TO THE JUMBOTRONS?
YEAH. THEY ARE.
WHAT IS IT?
THE HOSPITAL. JUNE'S ALONE IN THERE.

I TOLD YOU— SHE'S JUNE IPARIS! DON'T HURT HER! SHE'S WORTH A LOT OF MONEY!

OOOF!

UHN!
WHACK
COME ON! FOLLOW ME!

WAIT—WE'LL GET TRAPPED UP THERE!

TRUST ME!

YOU KNOW HOW TO FLY THIS THING?!

REMEMBER I SAID I GREW UP IN THE COLONIES?

I WAS A PILOT TILL I PISSED OFF MY SPONSOR!
WHOOOSH
YOU'D BETTER BUCKLE UP BACK THERE! I'M GONNA PUSH THIS THING TO THE MAX! WE'LL BE BACK IN REPUBLIC AIRSPACE IN A FEW MINUTES!
WE STILL HEADING FOR DENVER?
WH-WHAT'S GOING ON?
WE'RE HEADING FOR THE CAPITOL TOWER.
I'M GOING TO ANNOUNCE MY SUPPORT OF ANDEN TO THE REPUBLIC.

HANG ON TIGHT.
ANTI-AIRCRAFT
MISSILES INCOMING!

BWOOOOOOOOM
DENVER, COMING UP FAST! GET READY!

WHAT ARE YOU DOING?! IF WE TRY TO GO OVER THE ARMOR, THEY'LL SHOOT US DOWN!
I KNOW WHAT I'M DOING!

WHOOOOOOSH
SKREEEEEEE

I'LL TRY TO LAND US AS CLOSE TO THE CAPITOL TOWER AS POSSIBLE!

POK
POK
POK
POK

WE'VE GOTTA GET OUT OF HERE!
KAEDE!
KAE—
SHE'S DEAD!
COME ON!

WATCH OUT!
KOF!
BWOOOF
GET UPWIND OF THE SMOKE!
IS THAT DAY?
DID HE COME BACK IN A COLONIES JET?!

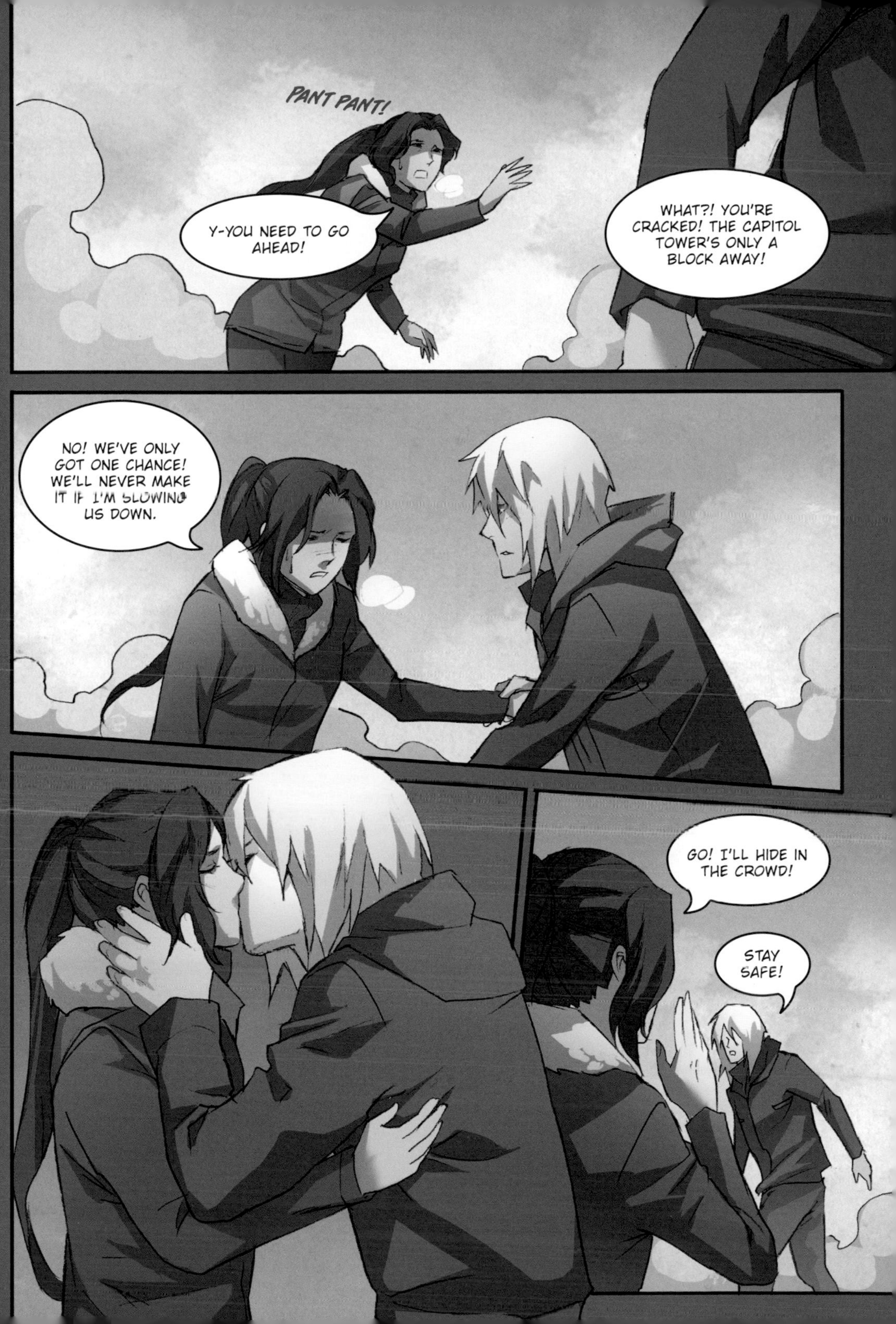

PANT PANT!

Y-YOU NEED TO GO AHEAD!

WHAT?! YOU'RE CRACKED! THE CAPITOL TOWER'S ONLY A BLOCK AWAY!

NO! WE'VE ONLY GOT ONE CHANCE! WE'LL NEVER MAKE IT IF I'M SLOWING US DOWN.

GO! I'LL HIDE IN THE CROWD!

STAY SAFE!

LOOK!
UP THERE!

DAY!
DAY!
DAY!
PEOPLE OF THE REPUBLIC! MY NAME IS DAY!
LIKE YOU, I'VE WATCHED MY FRIENDS AND FAMILY DIE AT THE HANDS OF REPUBLIC SOLDIERS. EACH OF US HAS RISKED OUR LIVES FOR THE COUNTRY WE HOPE ONE DAY TO HAVE!
THE NEW ELECTOR IS NOT YOUR ENEMY. ANDEN WANTS TO END THE TRIALS AND HELP YOUR FAMILIES!
HE WILL FIGHT FOR YOU IF YOU GIVE HIM THE CHANCE! I CAME HERE TONIGHT FOR YOU AND FOR HIM!

CONGRESS, I'M GIVING YOU AN ULTIMATUM! YOU'VE ARRESTED A NUMBER OF PATRIOTS FOR A CRIME YOU ARE RESPONSIBLE FOR. RELEASE THEM—ALL OF THEM—OR YOU'LL HAVE A REVOLUTION ON YOUR HANDS!
JUNE'S RIGHT. I DON'T WANT TO SEE THE REPUBLIC COLLAPSE.
DAY!
DAY!
I WANT TO SEE IT CHANGE.

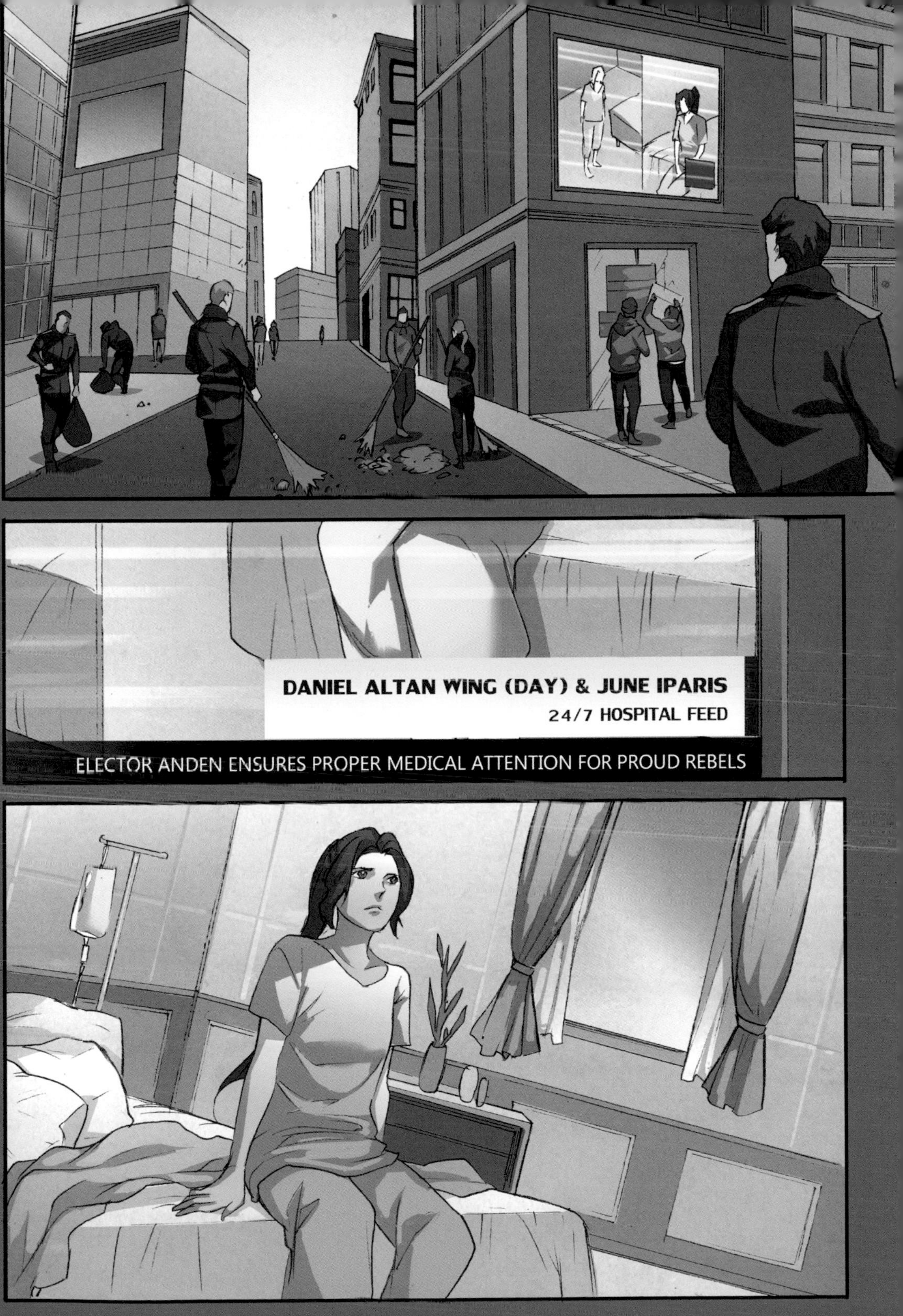

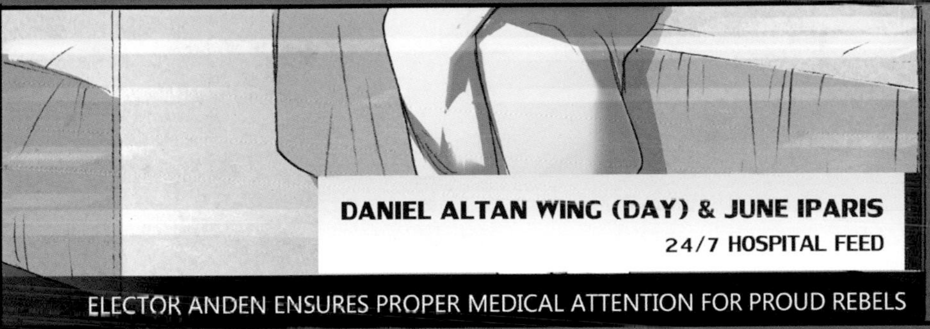
DANIEL ALTAN WING (DAY) & JUNE IPARIS
24/7 HOSPITAL FEED
ELECTOR ANDEN ENSURES PROPER MEDICAL ATTENTION FOR PROUD REBELS

https://therepublicnews.com/headline/news/14151/1abgr

Apps Project

Log In | Register Now

# THE REPUBLIC TIMES

## ELECTOR ANDEN OFFERS JUNE IPARIS PRINCEPS POSITION

WUFF

WOW. YOU LOOK INCREDIBLE.
WELL. PUBLICITY PHOTOS. YOU KNOW HOW IT GOES.

PICKED IT UP FOR YOU ON MY WAY HERE.

GASP!
RUBY'S YOUR BIRTHSTONE, RIGHT?

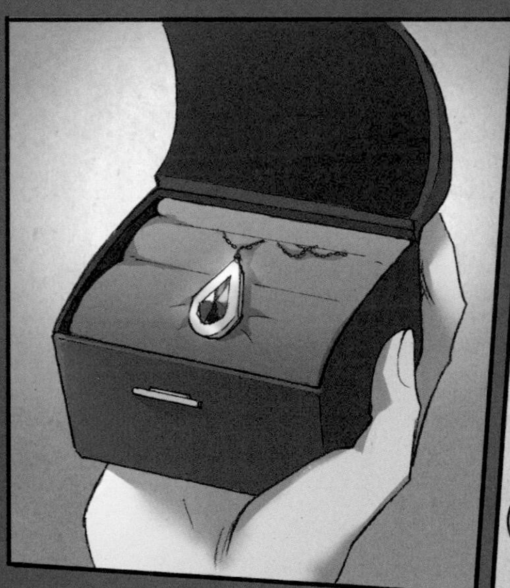

THANK YOU.
I STILL LIKE MY PAPER CLIP RING BEST.

I HEARD ABOUT THE JOB ANDEN OFFERED YOU.

I HAVEN'T DECIDED WHAT TO TELL HIM.
IT'S NOT LIKE IT'S A MARRIAGE PROPOSAL OR ANYTHING.

I CAME HERE TO TELL YOU TO TAKE HIS OFFER.
WHAT? WHY? WHAT ABOUT . . . ABOUT US? IT WOULD MEAN MONTHS AT A TIME AWAY . . . FROM YOU.
I'VE THOUGHT ABOUT IT A LOT AND . . . JUNE, WE JUST WEREN'T MEANT TO BE. TOO MANY THINGS HAVE HAPPENED.
SIGH
HIS FAMILY, HE MEANS. HE CAN'T FORGIVE ME FOR THE PART I PLAYED IN KILLING THEM.
HOW COULD I BE SO ARROGANT TO THINK THAT A COUPLE GOOD DEEDS COULD MAKE UP FOR THAT?
I NEED TO LET HIM GO. BUT I—
JUNE. LISTEN TO ME. TAKE THE JOB.

DAY—
NO. HEAR ME OUT. I MIGHT BE OKAY AT SPEWING SPEECHES AND WORKING A CROWD, BUT I DON'T KNOW ANYTHING ABOUT POLITICS. I'M NEVER GOING TO BE MORE THAN A FIGUREHEAD.
BUT YOU . . .
JUNE, YOU HAVE THE CHANCE TO CHANGE THINGS.
ALL RIGHT. I'LL LET ANDEN KNOW.
I'D BETTER GET GOING.

DAY, WAIT—
GOOD-BYE, JUNE.
WHIIIINE...

SIIIGH . . .
WE GOT BACK THE RESULTS ON YOUR SCANS.
RIGHT. YOU SAID YOU WERE JUST MAKING SURE THE COLONIES DIDN'T STICK ANY MONITORING DEVICES IN MY HEAD.
YES. WE DIDN'T FIND ANYTHING TO WORRY ABOUT . . . BUT WE RAN ACROSS SOMETHING ELSE.

WE SAW THIS NEAR YOUR LEFT HIPPOCAMPUS. WE THINK IT'S OLD, AND THAT IT'S BEEN WORSENING OVER TIME.
OUR . . . OUR RECORDS SHOW THAT YOU WERE EXPERIMENTED ON, AFTER YOU FAILED YOUR TRIAL. SOME TESTS WERE CONDUCTED ON YOUR BRAIN.
YOU . . . AH . . . WERE MEANT TO SUCCUMB QUICKLY . . . BUT YOU SURVIVED.
IT SEEMS THE EFFECTS ARE STARTING TO CATCH UP WITH YOU.
AND?
SIGH.
IT MEANS, DAY, THAT YOU'RE DYING.